29 to 31
A Book of Dreams

Kevin Staniec

For further information, please contact:
info@blackhillpress.com

ISBN-13: 978-0615905792
ISBN-10: 061590579X

Edited by William Brandon
Foreword by Corrie Greathouse
Artwork by Sami Viljanto

Printed in the U.S.A.

FOREWORD
Corrie Greathouse

Since childhood, I have toyed with the idea of keeping a record of my dreams. It has always seemed like a good idea, a way to recognize things in the light of day that I might not otherwise see. Despite this, I have always lacked the whatever-it-is that compels one to wrest themselves from half-sleep-haze of midnight to write their dreams. Myriad are the times have I woken in the middle of the night, saying

"I need to write that down. In the morning."

There are things in my life, specifically from my childhood, that, even as an adult, I am unsure are real. That is to say, I am not sure whether some of my childhood memories were dreamt. I live in a bit of a dream state. A slight disconnect between me and the rest of the world, a small tear somewhere in the fabric of reality is the space I feel most at home creatively and personally.

When Kevin told me about this book of dreams, I was intrigued. Burroughs had his dream book, but I had never known anyone who had actually kept a log every day for any significant length of time. Kevin was someone doing something I wished I could.

At the time, we were periodically corresponding via email: the letter of the 21st Century. When Kevin explained his Book of Dreams, I was inspired. His project moved me into my favorite space of disconnect. I responded, anticipating a wait of a week or two for a response, as had become our custom, but the response came within minutes:

"Have you ever written a novella"?
"No." I replied.
"Would you like to"?
"But what would I write about"? I wondered.
"About everything you just wrote to me."

With the launch of Black Hill Press, we saw the letter inspired by his Book of Dreams come to life in the life of the narrator in my novella Another Name For Autumn. Chapter One of the novella remains essentially untouched as the original correspondence I sent to Kevin. I allowed his Book of Dreams to carry me. I read it and allowed it to carry the narrator on her journey, as she reconciled her experiences with love, loss, and isolation; living in her own dream state, moving again among and into the world.

Some of these dreams may seem achingly familiar; I believe that is because when we dream, we are all the same. Allow these dreams to inspire you, allow them to move you, to carry you; perhaps they will help you remember dreams you have forgotten, and remind you to believe in miracles.

PREFACE
Kevin Staniec

At the conclusion of a three-year relationship I purchased an antique Smith & Corona from a stranger living in Riverside. This portable *Silent* from the early 1930's survived the Depression, and social, political and religious war while typing administrative reports, class assignments and love letters. I placed the typewriter on my nightstand and hit keys every morning, sometimes even before my eyes opened, documenting these dreams.

What started as a creative study of my unconscious developed into a therapeutic process through three stages of recovery — denial, anger, and acceptance. In his preface, Jack Kerouac wrote of his sleep journal, "Book of Dreams was the easiest book to write," but for me this project would be the most difficult three years of my life.

I was 29 when we broke up. I was 31 when I moved on.

29

~ 1 ~

I was sleeping when my mother handed me the phone, "Sounds important." It was a local radio station – their morning show. I answered, not wanting to talk, pacing perfect circles around my mind trying to figure out why they called. I was slow waking up, "Hello? How did you get my number?"

She was sitting on an armchair in the corner of my room. "He really liked me," moving to the foot of my bed, stopping to smile, "he liked me something awful before we eventually stopped seeing one another." She was talking over the person talking on the phone. I couldn't focus.

She pulled the sheets off my bed like a magician attempting to keep place settings on a table, "This shouldn't bother you. We're separated." I disconnected the line and walked outside. She followed, flirting for punctuation. It was annoying the way she did things. She reminded me of a little sister – always asking questions. I hate questions.

"Stop following me," I shouted, grabbing her forearm. "Stop! Please stop."

I was lying in bed again staring at my ceiling fan. It seemed to move like an hour hand, ever so slowly. Determined, the radio station continued calling. My phone kept ringing. I never answered.

~ 2 ~

My parents planned a religious retreat. They campaigned for celebrities to help prevent tourists from walking on the beach. Their crusade was ill-conceived and unsuccessful. Crowds gathered along the shore, ankle deep in sand. Everyone wore boonie hats with bucket flaps and painted their face with sunblock.

I was content sitting on a borrowed bicycle near an artificial dune built to prevent flooding. Steve Martin was the most recognizable advocate from the broadsheets. He was easy to laugh telling tales of ethnic foods. He pronounced everything incorrectly with a bad accent. I think he was just hungry. My parents didn't arrange for catering.

I left for the theater up Main Street. A friend of mine landed the lead in a musical about leaves. He never made it to the stage. I refused to applaud his understudy.

Later, my father yelled at me for not locking the bike up to a tree.

~ 3 ~

The entire neighborhood was preparing for a wedding. I did not know who was getting married, but a red rubber carpet was rolled out for the bridal chorus and the wedding march. Gardeners groomed plastic blades of grass. Servants spit-shined synthetic suits and varnished vinyl dresses. Forecasts predicted clean and warm weather.

Every second or so, I would remember to kiss the back of her neck. But it was obvious I was nervous about the paparazzi. "It's simple," she said. "Just start with a slight sidestep, and we're there."

I decided to step away.

I drove down dry abandoned roads bordered by desert. My windows were wide open and dust sifted through unrestricted, blanketing my car. Beige overwhelmed my senses. With my collar up, I shrugged my shoulders tight, ready to tear off the wheel.

My phone rang. It was an old friend from high school, "If you get to the party early, you have a chance at a free car." I eased up on the gas and paused a moment before responding, "I'm not quite sure you remember who I am. Did you dial the wrong number?" He hung up. I accelerated.

I watched television while waiting at a register in an empty food court. A maid mopped the checkerboard floor with soapwater buckets and refused to take my order. She was whistling the theme from "Love Story."

I ordered two palmfuls of trail mix. The lady behind the counter tried to charge me extra, "I'm not paying for the raisins!"

She smiled while giving me my change, "Did you know shredded coconut costs more than peanuts?"

For some reason, I found this hilarious.

~ 4 ~

"You can't give a horse lemonade, he'll never trust you," my brother said while scratching his hand across his chest, "probably end up kicking you as well." He walked out the front door, waving his arm at the wind as to not get caught by spider webs collecting under the arbor trellis. I wanted to ask him how much hair one can grow before it becomes too much hair, but I didn't.

Back in college, I didn't cut my hair for five months straight and the girls thought I had a lot of hair.

The next morning, I was sitting in the dining room signing bills or contracts. I was increasingly concerned with my signature. My handwriting was horrible. Every letter I wrote was wrong and didn't even spell my name correctly.

I attempted to erase the page, but it only made more errors. My friend, who was babysitting several kids while cradling a baby in her arm, said I could borrow her towel to wipe off the ink, but she failed to mention she had used that same towel earlier when painting. Primary colors smeared across my paper. Everyone around the table was laughing and telling jokes. Every punch line was about a dentist.

~ 5 ~

Gripping gallons of sky, ripping through threads of air, propelling forward, pulling hard-fast while leapfrogging wind tunnels, high jumping, catching armfuls of cloud. This is the only way I know how to fly, as I look down at friends. They walk upon fresh-cut lawns with box-shaped chalk lines. I decide to join them. One kid plays catch with himself. It's his birthday.

And at a music store, holding a 7-inch 45 close to my heart, the security guard wraps his massive arms around my small shoulders, "That's what it's about." Smiling, "That's what it's all about."

Many miniature instruments play hollow sounding symphonies in the back of my mind. I slow dance, off-tempo, single steps at a time, turning only to keep track of gravity. A man dressed like an Indian cuts in, "You dance like a cowboy, Cowboy."

My teacher approaches, sitting beside my desk. She is staring at my pants, disappointed. I look down to notice dry weeds all over my iron-creased khakis. Embarrassed, I quickly brush my hands down my thighs. She writes me a pass, "You really should wear another style of pants."

I get out my trapper-keeper and write down what she said.

~ 6 ~

The Angelus Church bell rings "Nearer My God to Thee." I must be late for class, but I graduated years ago. We cross paths as I find my way to the campus courtyard. She didn't recognize me.

I've had this dream before.

I approach a student balancing books while walking to class, "Have you read all of these?" His hair is bright red, his face, flushed from carrying everything from his locker. He levels me a look, "That's not what you asked me last time."

He remembers as well.

"Is this a dream?" I ask. He continues walking. I follow close behind, unnerved, "Why am I here?"

Direct, like a doctor, "Maybe these are side affects from chemotherapy?" I stop, heavy. "Your breathing is short and shallow, but nothing to be concerned about. You should be resting in bed… instead of wandering around here."

"Where is here?"

"Your thoughts, your memories…" He smiles, "Life has been good, everything will be fine."

"But why doesn't Stephanie recognize me? I want her to remember me." His books are gone. He places his hand on my shoulder.

I wake up crying and desperate for air. Stephanie lost her battle with cancer in 1998 and these dreams happen regularly.

~ 7 ~

It was a handmade town. The clouds reminded me of low-hanging dirt puddles in mud pockets overflowing with water and ready to spill. The wind was waiting outside walls, whistling through broken building breaks. It was a sully city of sawdust and shatter.

She sat small at an uneven round wooden table. Her feet would swing and kick between the legs of her chair. Mother washed dishes while staring out the window. She was watching the weather.

"When will I be able to dance again, mother?" her finger tracing the trim of her placemat.

The mother wipes her hands with her apron and turns to her child, "As soon as we can afford shoes to help teach you to breathe."

~ 8 ~

On the rear bench of a two-door, rust and tan, 68' Pontiac Bonneville convertible. Top down. Windows up. Nat King Cole crooning to the sky.

I think it's winter because I'm wearing a wool car coat and a houndstooth scarf. My brother drives with his long arm lazy over the wheel. Looking over his shoulder, he is talking about something while bouncing off lane lines, zigzagging down the narrow highway. "Dreams come a dream at a time," he says while approaching a stop sign. We don't stop.

We turn toward a small town that reminds me of the sixties. My brother wants something antique, "I just want to feel how it used to feel, when we were younger, when it didn't matter."

I was thinking about hand-wound Victrolas and collections of homemade 78's spinning jazz standards. The kind where chorus girls harmonize perfectly with your disposition.

As we turn another corner the radio finds a different frequency – Cole's 'Somewhere Along The Way' to Joplin's 'Solace'. I relax my head back, stretching my hands wide across the leather sofa seat. The clouds look like upside down snow hills.

~ 9 ~

My parents were lecturing me about relationships again. They didn't approve of my last girlfriend. "Your mother and I have been in love since 1966." My father, looking in his rear view mirror, "You're brother has been married for almost 6 years now, and tomorrow, you'll be 30. You don't have many other options." I shrugged it off as we approached the state line. Mexico wasn't my idea, but I had no choice. My dad parked the car, twisting back toward me, talking over his shoulder, "Good luck kid."

My mother got out of her seat to give me a hug and kiss my forehead, "Remember we're always proud of you." She smiled before sitting back beside my father. I watched them drive away, dust kicking out from under their tires. I turned around to see the border fence and took a deep breath…

~ 10 ~

In a large front yard, I play catch with a stranger beneath early autumn sycamore trees. I'm trying to convince him life is short, but I don't think he can hear me, so I shout, "Why stare at a cup of water, when you can look at the ocean?" I throw the baseball back with a smile.

He takes a moment before responding, "I'm just ready for something big to happen," and he drops the ball at his feet before walking away.

I open my suitcase and start packing, crying because I know – that was my last chance. And as a result of my behavior, my brother is fired from his job, my parents are eventually evicted from their house, the place where we grew up, and we're forced to live in our station wagon, the same car that got us here in the first place.

Disappointed, my mother asks, "Why would you even say that?" I look over at my brother, he seems all right with everything. Everything seems all right.

~ 11 ~

It was a floor lamp with a vintage step-switch. My grandfather made it for me as a gift. He handcrafted the shade using recycled stained glass.

Because my kitchen was dark I never cooked, and instead of eating at the dining room table I sat in the living room on the couch with a plate in my lap. I placed the lamp on the tile floor next to the stove. Finding an outlet, I removed the power cord connected to the toaster on my counter and plugged in the lamp. Somebody was watching me over my shoulder. It was a tall and slender man without a face. He was wearing crease-ironed slacks that were too short and black leather shoes with a thick layer of wax polish. I step down upon the push button and the light turns on. The bulb is bright and causes me to squint. As my eyes adjust I notice silhouettes of insects and small animals living near the floorboards of my cabinets. They seem hungry and frightened. I lean in closer to have a look when suddenly, a small spider crawls out from a crack in the wall. He is growing larger and chasing after me. His eight legs race up my body reaching for my stomach…

~ 12 ~

The lobby is filled with suits and gowns. Obviously I am dressed down for this occasion, but I don't seem to mind. On my left arm is the best friend of an ex-girlfriend from college. My right arm anticipates the arrival of my recent ex-girlfriend. I couldn't tell you why we are here or what we are celebrating, but champagne glasses toast regularly. "Sure feels like autumn," the best friend says while finishing her wine, red to red, lips to glass, Syrah to tongue.

As a waiter conducts the orchestra to play the first act waltz from 'Sleeping Beauty,' I turn around to find my date for the night has left me. I panic and push through the party searching for my recent ex-girlfriend, but I can't find her either, I'm not even sure she intended on attending. I am standing in the middle of the ballroom floor holding an empty glass of what was once filled with whiskey and ice and nobody is dancing. The crowd quiets, the music hollows, and then a hand touches my arm, "Hello," she whispers.

~ 13 ~

God works part-time at an antique shop. There is a sign outside that says "sale", but all he sells is history and his shelves are empty. He asked if I could move some sycamores closer to the shore because the tide was rising and the city had not yet learned how to drown. A girl at the end of the line was telling everyone, "The bus is leaving tomorrow, the bus will be leaving early in the morning," but my shirt reads 'thief' and this puts me in a precarious position.

~ 14 ~

The diner is called The Parasol. Orange, red, and tan umbrellas hang from the ceiling, upside down, with metal holes allowing light to drip onto the tables. I am sitting in a bright pink booth, my back facing the regulars who sit at the bar eating breakfast. I am staring past my reflection in the window at winter clouds. This season inspires me but always leaves me lonely. I can feel the cold through the glass.

My waitress is on a smoke break and hasn't once asked if everything was okay. I wasn't hungry so I disassembled my sandwich spreading the turkey, pickles, lettuce, and tomato, evenly across my plate. It starts raining and I pay my bill at the register.

When I returned the next day everything was gone—the diner, the umbrellas, the regulars, and the waitresses—all gone. The storm destroyed everything. All that was left were pink booths. "They say it was a hurricane," a man said while walking through the wreckage, "The city, she's flooded. I'm still trying to find my wife."

I wanted to find my waitress. I missed her. The wind was getting aggressive when my dad pulled up in the old family van, my mother sitting beside him. My brother slid the side door open, "Let it go," he shouted, "It's getting worse!" I didn't pay attention and sat in my usual seat, the weather coming down on me. While waiting for my waitress I started reading the menu.

~ 15 ~

She was whispering, leaning over my chest, her hands on my shoulders, holding herself up. I was shy and tried avoiding eye contact, nervous I'd forget my lines. Her hair fell tangled over her face; she was looking at me through a thin blonde curtain with green splashed hazel with ink blacks. Her stare was deep and unforgiving. But those lips, they were thin and they quivered. She was trying to tell me something, but I was fixated on ceiling with Mozart Number 21, Adagio A Major.

~ 16 ~

"We used to be laughter, we used to be happiness," I continue, even though she isn't listening, "we used to be that 'perfect' other couples were jealous of." I reach across the table and grab her wrist, "Are you listening?" She looks down at my hand then back across the highway toward the ocean. "Our hours were days… our days, weeks." A truckful of spring breakers peel out of the parking lot, bass bumping from their speakers. I take a second before continuing, "Just help me believe that this is hard for you too."

~ 17 ~

Barn board sidings cover his walls, his mattress stands upright against his closet, and drawers are left open with his clothing spilling onto the floor. Patrick sits on the carpet inside his empty bed frame listening to talk radio. Patrick stacks record jackets in crooked columns near his nightstand frisbeeing vinyl into unbalanced barricades near the door. Patrick, his hands stutter and tremble. Patrick is second-guessing. Patrick is hesitant; he is blue note. Patrick trades jazz for Bowie and Joel. Patrick is morning hair, all day and all night. Patrick is constant life and cigarette smoke. Patrick is Hotel Yorba, pacing with boat boots, rhythmically hitting his heal hard into the ground. Patrick is freckles, his face is smiling, he is nervous about smiling. Patrick, I wonder, why does music play you? What is it with these sounds that make you?

~ 18 ~

The river formed an oxbow lake. Soon after the stream was cut off from packet ships a retired machinist settled upon the land near the bottom of the U-shaped waters. Local natives called him Kapten. His men were heavily armed and miles of dipterocarp trees surrounded the area. Once you were in, you would never get out, unless you had something worth trading for.

I'm an aspiring photojournalist and first heard about Kapten while touring Indonesia. Rumor had it the old man controlled the waters because he was the only one left with a boat, and he burned everything used to transport goods. My guide introduced me to a scout who was familiar with the area. This was my last stop before heading home and my camera was running out of film.

We built a small punt from wood left behind by loggers and pushed our way along the bank. Traveling with us was a girl I met just outside of town. She was spontaneous by nature. Her stories were the kind shared by armchair tourists who dream of travel. I couldn't see them, but I could feel them, they followed us from behind the trees.

Kapten was waiting for us on an ornate settee. With his knife he split a durian on a tree stump and cut out a piece of its flesh. Kapten was wearing a safari helmet and had a beard that was long and coarse. The workers had stopped cutting trees and watched us as we approached. His men gathered, raising their rifles. I snapped a few photos of the people around the camp; their faces were full of fear, horror. Kapten had a menacing smile; it was the definition of evil. Our scout pulled out a gun and began to shoot warning shots into the air, but nobody moved, nothing happened. The old man laughed as we began to take on water, the wood of our boat splintered and expanded, the planks separated. The current was pulling us into the middle of the river when the Kapten stood up, and with the heel of his combat boot pushed his drift pram into the water. It was floating slowly toward us when he pulled out his pistol and shot a hole through its hull. This, our one hope for survival, our only hope to escape was sinking. Everybody watched us as we drifted into the current, drowning. Nobody was helping, nobody was moving. I took a picture…

~ 19 ~

My brother was president. I'm not sure how he was elected. I'm not sure I even voted for him. My dad and I helped move his belongings into the oval office while my mother shopped for new window dressings. We managed to fit everything into that small space—his bedroom, his kitchen, and his garage. Afterward, our family was given the token tour. I was bored and walked ahead of the guide. My parents caught up with me later near the courtyard gardens where an architect was lecturing about the origins and history of each individual flower. We traveled down a narrowing path of vertical hedges that lead us toward a lobby, "This reminds me of Paris, Las Vegas," I said. My brother shot me a look. He can do that now, he's the President. My mother was nervous and asking a lot of questions, "Don't you think this is a lot of responsibility?" I'm not sure she voted for him either. We stopped at the food court. My father sat at a cafeteria table— he seemed embarrassed, staring up at clouds painted on the ceiling. I'm not sure this is what he wanted for my brother.

~ 20 ~

We're hosting a party and we invited everyone from the retirement home next door. A friend of mine from the office brought a large Tupperware bowl filled with gravy. He hoped someone would bring turkey, but nobody did. This was typical of him. A larger gentleman confined to a wheelchair, his big belly resting on his lap, was angry with everyone and everything. He rolled up to the food table and locked his wheels. Using the punch ladle, he lazily slopped lumps of gravy down his throat—scooping spoonfuls, slurping as if it were soup. Gravy was spilling everywhere, "somebody should be watching him," I said to my co-worker, concerned. But, everyone was watching him; it was disgusting. You just couldn't take your eyes off him. Suddenly, he began to choke, violently. It was just too much gravy, filled him right up. One of the nurses ran toward him holding a box of instant guacamole mix, a rubber spatula in her hand. She began force-feeding the guacamole powder into his mouth. Unfortunately, he didn't make it. He died in our dining room. The mood turned melancholy, but we had to continue with the party, he would have wanted it that way.

~ 21 ~

My eyes open, my head between pillows, my body tangled in blankets. The ceiling seems further than usual, more distant. Old shirts pushpinned to the wall cover my window, preventing day from entering the room. I hear rain outside and I want to close my eyes, but it's Monday and I have to get up and go to work. Sun shines through cloud, through window, through shirt—orange, blue, green—a cotton/polyester stained-glass morning. I finally force myself out of bed. My muscles ache as I stretch, reaching for the top of my fingers, trying to find the tip of my toes. Scratching a spot below my neck, between my shoulders, where my sheets left a crease with a trail tracing over my shoulder. Pounding head, cracking bones, each insignificant step an insignificant victory as I walk to the living room. My mother is watching the weather, "Morning, Sunshine. Be sure to bundle up before going outside." I stand beside her, both of us in our pajamas, watching thin mists of rain dissipate before touching the grass. Strands of icicle lights hang from our roof soffit. Each little white bulb reminds me of a frozen drop of rain. This is nice.

~ 22 ~

A piano in the middle of an old Oriental rug. Dust on its keys.
A composition book open on its music rack. The wood is
chipped and cracked and stained from sweat and grease. I can
still hear music. The last chord, the last hit of its hammer
against string—it is still vibrating.

~ 23 ~

I was walking around the store when I noticed behind the front counter there was a picture of me taped to the wall. I approached a manager, somewhat disturbed, "That's a picture of me, what's it doing up there?" The manager wasn't exactly sure how it got there, but he smiled and shook my hand, "Congratulations, you finally did it."

$\sim 24 \sim$

It was just another scene in another scripted love story. Rehearsals were scheduled a week prior to shooting. It was early summer and Matt was staying with his girlfriend, Melia, who had a place near the beach. Lauren arrived a day late and unpacked at her hotel nearby—top floor with a balcony, just as her contract required. At night she read lines with a glass of red wine.

Melia was always on set, and on the last day of blocking, Matt finally introduced her to Lauren. Awkward would be an understatement. Melia watched Matt and Lauren practice their first kiss all morning—by the end of the day, they were no longer acting. She confronted Matt back at his trailer and left later that night.

"Actors ready?" the director shouted as Matt checked his mark. "Action!" Matt pulled Lauren in for their first kiss.

~ **25** ~

My brother packs his suitcase. My mother rubs my back, "relax, everything will be fine." She knows I hate planes. My father loads our luggage into the car.

On the plane, propellers begin to turn. I can't sleep. I unbuckle my belt and run back down the aisle. Passengers are worried, some frightened. I pull the airplane door open to notice we are flying above the clouds. I fall through thick smoke rising from a fire below.

~ 26 ~

Four of us stand in a glass elevator—a gentleman in a three piece suit holding a briefcase and umbrella, an elderly lady wearing a floral house dress holding the hand of her granddaughter, and the elevator operator in uniform. "Where are we going?" I ask the man working the buttons. "Up," he answers.

~ 27 ~

He squeezes past without acknowledgement. "'Scuse me!" I said, punching the philistine in the stomach. The sky split along the horizon as the world widened along the equator. Everyone was staring at me as the room split, as if I had something to do with this. Catching his breath, this sudden gentleman stepped toward me, presumptuously, "May I help you?" I was ready to teach him a lesson in manners using my fists when my brother stepped in, immediately grabbing the unsophisticate around the ankles and swinging him like a propeller before slamming his face into a brick wall. "Sleep tight," my brother said.

We quickly hopped into a car and drove around the block, turning right back into the same spot in the same parking lot. We vaulted from our seats and sprinted for a darkened backstreet. The alley narrowed toward a small door with no handle—my brother didn't stop running and lowered his shoulder into its hinges, breaking it clean off its frame.

We were suddenly in the middle of an enormous stone stadium. It reminded me of the Roman Coliseum, only ten times taller. The crowd began to chant as roses were tossed into the arena.

~ 28 ~

Walking in shadows of elm branches. Leaves falling into the street like heavy river stones. Autumn reminds me of crying. Crying reminds me of spring. I can't remember the order of things, but I continue pulling weeds from pavement cracks, cutting flowers from yard bushes and carving names into tree trunks.

At the end of the block my friends wait for me. "You shouldn't be here," one of them whispers. Everyone is thirteen again, except I seem older, much older. "What are you talking about?" I ask, "What's wrong with watching the sun set?" I motioned to the clouds swelling overhead, they were emitting a variety of surreal color hues, but my childhood companions didn't seem interested. They didn't care that night was upon us and they didn't budge from their hard stance, arms crossed, muscles flexed.

Suddenly, Teresa was walking across a neighbor's lawn. She was smiling ever so tenderly, her face exactly the way I remember it from our first date, but I hadn't seen her since we separated. Before we could even say hello, kids hiding in trees, started throwing pebbles at us. I grabbed Teresa's hand and we started running back in the other direction—fist-sized garden-rocks breaking into the concrete beneath our feet. Teresa was hit. She stumbled to the ground as rocks continued to fly past us. "Are you alright?" I ask, trying to help her up. She looked up at me, her face covered with blood, I hardly recognized her. "Everything is fine… isn't it?"

~ 29 ~

A zip-locked plastic square. A bag, small, slippery and clear.
It is safety-pinned to the breast pocket of that corduroy blazer,
through that pinstriped lining. This poly bag used to hold
extra buttons, but was empty because I had already lost
several buttons elsewhere—and this jacket has seen a needle
and thread many times before, and the sleeves are uneven and
one arm is tighter around the wrist than the other. And my
palm is open.

Zip-lock, plastic, clear, filled with cocaine or powdered
sugar... hide that secret in your drawer, behind your
underwear and socks, inside a wooden box. My dad walks in
the room, holding the folded laundry, "Whats'ya got there?"

~ 30 ~

My father is folding laundry in the family room while watching Sunday football. The afternoon sun sits lazy on our patio as a still wind wanders through our sliding screen door. I am pacing back and forth, creating patterns in the rug while text messaging with two girls. We don't have the time to use verbs and we disregard all vowels. "Sit down, Kevin," raising his voice, "The floor needs washing, and you're making me nervous. Watch the game and tell me the score when it's over." He leaves the room with a mop and pail. I'm not wearing socks and my feet are getting cold. I shout down the hallway, "Dad! I need socks without holes!" He doesn't respond. The game ends, 21 to 22.

~ 31 ~

June was the same every year and summer camp was far from home. Our parents drove us out of town, away from friends, and we were forced to fit in with a bunch of strangers. They dropped us off, our life packed in duffel sacks and hanging loose off our shoulders. My first instinct, after counselors separated my older brother and I, was to find familiarity or at least someone else also looking for familiarity. I found Craig.

We were staying in a filthy motel with crooked walls and cracks in the ceiling. The room was filled with rollaway beds dressed with itchy wool blankets and dust-covered lamps that smoked when turned on. They were training us to dream, but I couldn't sleep. A couple next door was having angry sex— their iron headboard banging against our wall. I could hear springs breaking. I couldn't sleep.

The sound of a gunshot rings in my head. My eyes widen as I stare through the keyhole below the doorknob. The deadbolt is locked, but I can see shadows running down the hall. Everyone evacuates immediately and we are lead to the gymnasium. Our advisor blows his whistle, "You're all gonna run until someone admits to firing a gun!" He blows his whistle again and we all run, from baseline to charity stripe and back, baseline to half court and back. Coach pulls me aside, "Your parents are dead." He places his hand on my head and messes up my hair.

Craig and I walked home. When we arrived, we went straight for the kitchen because we were hungry. When I opened the cabinet a spider jumped out at me…

~ 32 ~

Teresa had put on some weight since we were together. It was raining as she walked down the street and caught my eye. She wore a headset, probably listening to opera; she never noticed me intently following the feeling of recognition. My friend Morgan was with me as we followed her. "I've finally found Jesus," he said, which was odd because I knew he was robbing banks and thieving trains. He continued talking, but I wasn't listening. I was just waiting for her to turn around. If she looks back at me, she still loves me. She turns around, Morgan and I smile.

Morgan and I purchased tickets to a matinee with a friend from middle school. The four of us hopped from screen to screen, watching film previews. It was still raining and everyone was at the theater. We bumped into a friend from high school and another girl I'd recently been seeing. The row went boy, girl, boy, girl, boy—and then Teresa walked down the aisle and sat beside me—girl. I tried to kiss her.

~ 33 ~

If I wrote a story about you, it would involve birds. Birds that sing. Birds that fly. I would handwrite this story in 17th century cursive and title it "Kingfisher."

~ 34 ~

Believe me when I say, "I would love to be an honest man."
Believe me when I say, "I want to believe her." But some days
are longer than others and I realize it would be impossible to
listen to every single word. It'd be nice to just dance with you,
as fast and as small as humanly possible, where ever we want,
music or not.

~ 35 ~

This morning has been tough for me. Tough because I love her, love because it's tougher.

30

~ **36** ~

She is half asleep, idly scratching the same spot on my back and talking about erasers — it is cold, gray, and raining.

I am cleaning, preparing my apartment for writing. I don't want to let the admiral down. I'm meeting him at an abandoned warehouse, sometime early tomorrow morning or late in the afternoon.

A short, balding Italian wearing a tweed turtleneck sweater was waiting for me in the lobby. He was recently hired as the back-up bouncer at a local dive bar. He was honored.

Two girls helping with a fashion show apologize for being late. The cuter of the two always has a story to tell.

I can't focus because nobody seems prepared for their auditions. I turn on the house lights and exit out the black-box theater backdoor.

~ 37 ~

I'm sitting on a driveway in a cul-de-sac. On a reporter's notepad I write I DON'T WANT TO LET YOU DOWN in all caps. I'm only a quarter of the way into it and already, I've forgotten three quarters of thought. The garage door opens behind me, barely missing my head on its upswing. In one move, Tim skids his bike onto the sidewalk while flipping his kickstand. He removes his helmet, "That's right!" Tim is a large individual standing 6 foot 7 inches and weighing around three hundred pounds. "I'm late again." His smile reveals a mouth full of braces with red rubber bands.

The neighbors are organizing a football game at the park around the corner. I'm in a bad mood and I don't want to play, "I'm not depressed, I'm just sad." Two captains pick teams. Somehow it ends up boys versus girls. Police patrol the block. An undercover cop is walking an undercover dog.

I am in bed with an ex-girlfriend. She is annoying as usual. We start fooling around—hugging, rolling—when she notices her roommate has invited guests over. My ex is instantly distracted. I want to leave when a slender fellow enters her room. He smiles. She smiles. I pull her covers off the bed and she is naked. She doesn't care. Neither of them seem bothered. I walk out of the room dragging her sheets along the floor behind me.

~ 38 ~

My friend was arrested in Baja for racing. I was jealous and bought a bus ticket for Mexico. Nobody was on that route and the seats were empty. I sat in the back staring out the window.

A friend was helping me build something in my parents' garage. He had an idea, "We have an extra room at the gallery; this should be an installation." I thought about it for a second, "We could use my Polaroids to decorate the walls."

Jack, a gallery director, was in my bedroom on my phone filing my papers.

~ 39 ~

I grab the double-barreled shotgun from my gym bag, "only three bullets left." My .45 Colt fits in the waistband of my tracksuit. In my sock drawer, I have a vintage six-shooter, which was a gift from my twenty-first birthday. I bring it…just in case.

Nervously I pace at the crown of a bridge—gunfire and screams in the distance—when suddenly, everything stops. Silence. An old man with a small group of kids calmly walks past me. He tips his hat as they cross to the other side.

Something about a robbery, a rollercoaster, and a suicide.

The buildings on campus are cold and constructed of brick and ivy. Rows of oak chair desks square the classroom. Our teacher, who doesn't seem to be teaching, speaks with a thick Southie accent. Classmates exaggerate their every move and dramatically interact with one another like a daytime soap opera. A girl with freckles across her cheeks sits in front of me. She loves the East Coast, however she hates the long commute from San Diego. I spend my break with a foreign exchange student who speaks broken English. He takes heavy drags of his cigarette and continuously nods his head in agreement. I ditch class for a friend who wants to show me his photos from the weekend. Every picture looks the same, except for a slight change in the weather. I drive him home through heavy rain and traffic. Drivers rear end one another creating piles of cars several stories high. We take a different route.

~ 40 ~

He was old with silver hair. His sunglasses were always on and he only wore Hawaiian shirts. "Pleasure meeting you," he said with his hand open for a proper shake. I shared my story about reading his story in the paper, "I wanted to meet you and learn more about your company, which is why I'm here." I also told him about myself and my company and was dropping names left and right. He smiled, "Like butter." I thought he said, like butter, but I wasn't sure, "What was that you said?" He repeated, "Like butter." I followed him outside where his friend was waiting in a convertible Volkswagen Bus. I asked for their business cards and they both asked for mine. I was nervous and excited, and struggled to find the right card in my wallet. My wallet was filled with cards, hundreds of cards, and I also didn't want him to notice the condom hidden in the fold. I dropped collections of cards onto the ground when he noticed one he liked, "I like this one," and I handed him a couple more cards as well. He invited me to a meeting the very next day. I invited my brother because I wanted him to be there with me.

All four of us were sitting in a peddle-boat in the middle of a lake. I was disappointed; I wasn't peddling. Suddenly, an enormous submarine surfaced from beneath us. Both the businessman and his friend were laughing, "Welcome aboard!" And just like those old situation comedies from the seventies, we were frozen on television with credits rolling. Everyone laughing, our little boat balancing on the deck of the submarine.

~ 41 ~

I was lazy, lying in the grass near the foul line, complaining about the weather. I walked off the field after arguing with a family friend who was sitting in the bleachers.   The gymnasium doors were open and I stepped onto the basketball court. It brought back memories. I was disappointed. Kim and I were walking through the front gate at Disneyland. Together, we passed Main Street toward the toiletries aisle. Shopping carts crowded the sidewalks as holiday shoppers bargained for deals. Kim was impressed with Walt's keen business savvy. She wanted to buy everything. I hate crowds and pushed through to the other side—impatiently shoving anything in my way.

~ 42 ~

My brother is outside, running after a cat, when someone knocks on our door. I am sleeping with a girl from my past when the doorbell rings. I reel out of bed with my pillow, blankets and sheets, dragging behind me. When I open my eyes, my grandparents, my parents, and my neighbors are waiting in the living room and shout, "Surprise!" My brother, out of breath, comes running in holding the cat, "I didn't know we had a cat." We don't. My grandmother, placing her hand on my elbow, "Did you hear what happened?" My father interrupts, "It was late last night..." The cat escapes, again, and runs past the girl from my bedroom, who is now leaning against the hallway doorframe. She is wearing my favorite shirt and tying her hair back with a rubber band.

The world is under construction. Freeways spin endlessly in overlapping circles that scrape the sky. Every five feet there is a hazardous roadblock with hard hat officials holding blueprint plans mapping political and religious boundaries.

I hike for days over broken piles of timber, steel, and concrete that peak over the city. I remember that moment at the top looking down on the Santa Ana Freeway. This is the first time I've seen the horizon in decades. The sunrise reminds me of possibility. My alarm goes off.

~ 43 ~

The neighborhood where I grew up basically disappeared. My high school was destroyed. My college campus had been demolished—buildings reduced to scrap piles that were looted for metals. The landscape is deteriorating and dying. Using a piece of rebar for balance and protection, I walk narrow trails formed by scavengers. I am searching for answers. We anticipated the affects of global warming and climate change and how it would ultimately alter our planets atmosphere, but nobody could have predicated the consequences this would have on our solar system. The planet stopped spinning and the sun dried. The world population dropped from nine billion to 600,000 in less than three years. Water was regulated to specific regions and food rapidly became scarce. While digging for more resources we built small cities within the mantle region below the earths crust. Drilling hasn't stopped since we found new energy and nutrients in the Earth's outer core, but recently the temperature within the inner core has been unpredictable causing "beats," or earth echoes. I continue to travel, searching, and I won't give up until I find her.

~ 44 ~

My parents had guests in the living room. It looked as if everyone was asleep. The street was lined with cars, but my car was stolen. I still had my keys in my pocket. My friend Todd was double-parked. I began turning his steering wheel with my key chain—like a remote control. Every car on the block started turning and bumping into one another—it was all my fault. My father ran outside just as Todd crashed through our driveway gate. Todd got out of his car, "You play a good game, Staniec!" and walked away. Rain began to fall down the street near Jeremiah's house. He was outside painting his front door as water washed away every stroke of his brush. It was getting colder and darker. I sat down on the curb, waiting to be picked up, watching water run rapidly down the city drain. Brian walked across the street and sat down beside me, "She was beautiful, wasn't she?"

~ 45 ~

"My tears taste like salt." "Everything will be all right," my coach said, convinced his signature is better than mine—and it is.

My family is visiting me as we shoot on location in Morocco. Everything is calm on set after I sell an actress on the idea of using a production assistant.

I continue changing my clothes, preparing for a family vacation, but no matter what I wear I still look like a samurai. So I decide it's best to also walk like a samurai. We pile into the Aerostar and drive against the sun, past gymnasiums filled with kids playing basketball. Getting my brothers attention, "I've played there before." He gets out of the van to stretch his legs. My brother hasn't played basketball in years, but he seems determined to join a game.

I'm on a bus debating the aesthetics of Italian Neorealism with a child prodigy. "Cinematically," he says, "it's the intellectual's moving picture, and I've grown quite fond of the absence of reality." He isn't making sense, but I try to keep up anyway, "In my magazine, we do interviews..." Everyone on the bus turns to look at me, strangely.

~ 46~

I wake up and walk to the restroom. Flush. Outside, the sky is still dark. When I open the front door and my father is standing there. "Why are you still here?" I ask. "I have a dentist appointment this morning." I fall back into bed.

I kneel beside my bed with my hands clasped tightly together. I close my eyes and pray. My dad taps on my window, he is smiling. He walks toward my mother who is working in the garden. He whispers something in her ear and she turns to look at me, she is smiling.

I wake up. I pray, "May the sacred heart of Jesus be adored, glorified, loved and praised throughout the world now and forever. Sacred heart of Jesus, please pray for us. Saint Jude, worker of miracles, please pray for us. Saint Jude, helper of the hopeless, please pray for us."

I'm shooting hoops in an empty gym with my friend Mark. Last time I played basketball with him, I broke is hand. He has several screws in his hand because of me. I turn on the radio, scribble some thoughts on paper, and close the notebook. I close my eyes.

I wake up—open my eyes. I start writing in my notebook. I turn on the radio.

~ 47 ~

China. Royalty. Spring, 1983. I am sitting in the bleachers watching a soccer game. My suit is pressed and creased and my shoes are shined. My tie, my pocket square, and my socks all match. I am business class. Corner kicks are life defining.

Flying over San Francisco.

I am in a trailer park standing on the doorstep of an old mobile home.

Watching spring training baseball and my couch seems small. Foul ball.

I gave her my piano. I wonder if she ever plays.

~ 48 ~

The beach is beautiful this time of year. Hours later, I'm still sitting on the sand watching the ocean. A few friends walking along the shore stop to make small talk. I haven't seen Megan since graduation and I convince her to stay. Josh also sits with us, he has sun tan lotion all over his face, "You never know on these overcast days." It's Austin's birthday and I didn't bring a present. I always forget to bring gifts. The entire beach is looking for Austin; his family hasn't seen him for hours. I am sunbathing in a chaise lounge beach chair. His mother asks if I know where Austin is…I join the search party. Nonchalantly, I walk toward the pier. I climb a support beam and hang over the water, slowly inching out to sea during rising tide. Why do I think Austin would be under the pier? I don't know. And I don't find him.

Josh, Megan and I are walking around the parking lot when an old RV pulls up beside us. The driver is wearing a captain's hat, "This Winnebago is for sale and I know you're in the market for a Winnebago." I had to admit, he was right. I said goodbye to Megan and hopped aboard. The inside looked like a house. I was inspecting the amenities to make sure everything was in working order when the captain made an announcement over the PA, "But have you seen the view?" I turned to look out the window and noticed, somehow, that we were now in the mountains. He laughs as he parks, "How did I do that, you ask? Let's take a walk." As soon as I open the door, we are now in the desert. "It's yours if you want it, no questions asked." I take another look at the RV before making a decision and notice he has a baby anteater rolling around on the carpet. The carpet is covered in ants. "I'll pass, thanks for the ride." And then I walked into the desert.

We're eating at the dinner table. My parents want to know about my day. I tell them everything, spilling wine everywhere as I elaborate with my hands.

~ **49** ~

On the run, on the road, sitting behind the wheel of an antique Ford. Torn jeans, dirty white tee, and a six-pack sitting behind the driver seat. I finish my second can and throw it out the window.   I haven't shaved in weeks and I don't even recognize my own reflection in the rear view mirror. The wheels are rolling on an empty tank as I slowly pull to the side of the road and dirt kicks up around me. It's hot and wind travels triumphantly across the open plain. AM radio is the perfect passenger for a drive across country—I take my time finishing another beer and tossing the empty can out the window. A gentleman on a motorcycle pulls up beside me, "Need some help?" I tell him I can take care of these beers by myself just fine. He flashes his badge. I open another can. "You'll have to come with me."

In my cell, I stare at concrete blocks that square the corners around me. The cement has been painted over several times and sweats in this heat. I'm planning a prison break.

A group of us run through the forest, chased by dogs, cops and trucks—the town has come together to round us up.

CUT TO: My agent sits me down to discuss my autobiography. "It'll sell," he claims, "everyone loves an adventure." I pull a revolver from my pant pocket and shoot him in the face. Blood splashes onto the camera lens. Red always seems redder in black and white. He was crying before I pulled the trigger, reciting the names of famous authors who found celebrity writing about their lives.

CUT TO: A cellmate is shot in the back and falls face first into a creek. I am hiding behind a thick oak tree deep in the woods. "Shit, I just shot my lawyer in the face." One of the prisoners, from Japan, finds his way through the brush, past security and baggage claim. He turns to smile; suddenly, he is shot by a civilian sitting on a bench reading the paper. Airport police toss his body onto the conveyor belt with a toe tag guiding him home.

I light my last cigarette before raising my hands into the dry summer air. They called me cowboy, saying I was some kind of rebel, an outlaw—and that was fine with me; I didn't care much anyway.

I stare at concrete blocks that square the corners around me, writing my thoughts with a pencil on paper. I thought I should start at the beginning, "And there she was…"

~ 50 ~

Josh and I are lost in a mall. We circle consumer crowds while debating the current situation with our government and what little we know about our economy. As we turn a corner, past the food court, I notice a natural history themed kiosk. An elderly gentleman who owns the small shop welcomes us at his Dutch door. The room is the size of a closet; the main wall is covered with miscellaneous cupboards. I recognize the owner from somewhere, but I can't seem to place it. I feel as though he has been in my dreams before. He helps Josh search for something as the girl behind the counter is looking for a map. She is awkward, cute and I think she's flirting with me in a clumsy, yet somehow—seemingly—graceful manner. I find all of this amusing. Ever since I was a child, I had always wanted a guide to the stars, but she couldn't seem to locate anything about our skies. She turns to the old man for assistance. He gives her a tiny Victorian key. She opens a cabinet concealing a drawer that holds a safety box. They work together to unfurl a large roll of paper onto the countertop. The old man carefully sweeps dust off the artifact with an archeology brush to reveal a detailed blueprint of space, he smiles, "We've talked about this before, haven't we?"

~ 51 ~

The wedding was beautiful. It was a perfect day. The sun was hanging low and soft over the trees and everyone was dressed for the occasion in pearl whites and powder blues. I attended the ceremony and sat in the back of the chapel. I didn't recognize anyone from either side of the aisle and I did not know the bride or the groom. The couple seemed enamored with one another as they exchanged their vows. He was nervous, with his hands together behind him, pushing his chest out and his shoulders back. She was taking deep controlled breaths, attempting to hold her tears. The priest, at the altar, opened his bible as guests sat anxiously and somewhat uncomfortably in the wood plank pews. And then, the confessional exploded, fire and debris fragmented through the pulpit and crashed through the congregation. Bodies fell to the floor and shrapnel shot through suits and skin creating clouds of blood that painted the room pink—flower petals floating in the air. Then silence.

I'm okay and pull myself up from the ground. When walking up the aisle I notice a kid playing with a jigsaw puzzle on the carpet in the foyer.

~ 52 ~

Walking a winding dirt road through hill and farm. Pushpin trees dot the horizon with a decorative green. My friend snaps a few shots of an abandoned woodshed as he points toward a house near the creek, "That's the place... property ends at the pass. Animals come with it as well as the tractors." I notice a terraced area in the shadow of the mountain covered with tractors, there seem to be hundreds of them, "Do they still work?" "Of course," he continues walking down a rail fence path where we meet two ranch hands that work for a local breeder. I think they're brothers because they simultaneously dry their brow with their right hand using red bandanas.

~ 53 ~

My room is small and cold. I sneak my friend Priscilla into my bed and remove her clothing. The bed is wet. I think she wet the bed. I get up to clean the sheets and start a load of laundry. As I reach for a slice of strawberry pie, I am told about the peach cobbler, "I'd much rather wait for the peach cobbler."

~ 54 ~

Sitting on a dusty couch with dirty pillows. Billows of memory fill the air when I move. Everyone leaves the room. Sierra sits on the opposite end of the love seat, leaning against the armrest. I am sad and I apologize, when suddenly I don't trust her. I need to make copies but the office is a mess, the printer is out of ink, and the computer isn't working.

She cried while walking down the street.

~ 55 ~

The colder the night gets, the less I remember. Josh and I are playing in the backyard with friends from middle school, but it is almost impossible to understand what anyone is saying. It starts raining. It starts flooding. We throw dirt on the ground to absorb the water. We lay carpet on the floor inside to cover the mud. I help control a crowd at some seminar. Megan isn't paying attention to the lecture. She asks if I want to play tag, "We were once playground lovers, sandbox dating. Let's go down the slide again, together." My parents are late to pick me up and I still can't understand what anyone is saying. I feel disconnected, I feel lost. I continue looking for a broom.

~ 56 ~

I am sitting in the rear-facing backseat of my mother's old station wagon. The windows are down and I am staring at a cloud. My father is sick and sleeping soundly in the passenger seat. My wife is riding with her family. She should be sitting beside me. My mother continues to drive as thunderstorms strike in the distance.

~ 56 ~

~ 57 ~

Winter in Chicago. The howling air is heavy and wheezing—
wind slapping you across the face. The white sun, reflecting
off wet layers of snow and ice, seems flat but sharper than the
sun in California. I sit in the living room playing cards with
my cousins. The morning is quiet as my mother and
grandmother prepare dinner. When my grandfather was
around, we'd play in his toolshed or pick up apples that fell
from the trees in the backyard.

I sit in the corner, on the carpet, nervously playing with loose
threads. My cousins are at my side, "Everything will be just
fine." I think my father died. I leave for the kitchen to read an
article in the paper. I find a story about my friend Aaron with
a photo of him working in his studio. For some reason I am
troubled by this and turn the page.

~ 58 ~

It was my father's hand-me-down suit—high on the ankles, short around the wrists, tight in the waist. Waiting for the receptionist to notice me, I read a copy of my resume, whispering each word under my breath. An instrumental rendition of Led Zeppelin's *The Rain Song* softly plays in the background. "Kevin, please come with me," the secretary leads me down a narrow hall into a small room filled with computers. She sets me up in front of a monitor, "Answer the questions to the best of your ability. Good luck." The smell of her perfume lingers long after she leaves. I don't like tests. I click as fast as I can wherever I can. I finish the exam in under three minutes—the exam is expected to take three hours. I walk back to the waiting room, whistling *Over the Hills and Far Away*, and exit out the front door.

~ **59** ~

Everyone is sitting in an ancient stone amphitheater carved steep into a coastal cliff. The ocean seems promising, the waves crash with consistency, but nobody listens to the protest of a speaker who claims, "Rioting is the only viable solution!"

~ 60 ~

A charming little house was built in the hollow knot of a redwood—high and hidden along a haunting stretch of forest. Elegant oriental rugs decorated the hand-woven rattan wood walls and floors. A deep-rooted gramophone, now living within the tree, turned nocturnes at half speed. Paper shade candles hung from branches emitting a subtle-toned light. Women crocheted warm winter blankets using animal hair and plant threads. The old man smiled, he could tell I was hungry. He taught us about art and the wind. He used his stave for a cane, and asked if I would accompany him to scavenge for food. I pocket a couple Sial stones for protection.

~ 61 ~

I walk Hell Gate toward Astoria, occasionally taking pictures of the horizon around me. It's been raining since I left the South Bronx and I finally find shelter in a local bookstore. They have my art magazine on a shelf designated for *Travel*. It doesn't seem to be selling well, so I decide to purchase a copy—positive reinforcement. I step out onto the back porch and stand beside an empty rocking chair that rocks with the wind. The clouds seem frightened of the weather to come. I use my cell phone to call friends. Nobody is home, but their answering machines, momentarily, keep me company. I decide a documentary would be the best direction for discussing my depression. I hope it ends okay.

~ 62 ~

I sit in the 'Poetry' aisle at Either/Or on Aviation in Hermosa Beach. It always seems to be raining when I visit this bookstore. I'm holding a cup of coffee or a cup of tea and re-reading my favorite line from my favorite book on meditation. I ask a worker why my story was placed in the children's section. "It's because it comes with a free shirt, and kids love free shirts," he continues shelving books. Politely, I ask a manager to please place my work in the *Travel* section of the shop, "It makes sense. I promise." He says something about Silverstein, Seuss, and Saint-Exupery as I walk away. I find a local author who binds his books by hand. I purchase his book, read his book, and gift his book to a friend.

~ 63 ~

Mom and dad sit at the dining room table playing with frames. I implore, "Use another image, Dad." I'm upset because he's trying to fit a photo I took into a frame with a stack of pictures. I begin to tell my mother about a photographer who curated an entire show with white—white mattes, white frames, white walls, white lights… she snaps back at me, "I already have my mind made up."

~ 64 ~

We're moving into a new house. It's a single story ranch-style home with several rooms and a backyard the size of a football field. I stand on the back patio with my dad, staring at the telephone lines, the electrical towers, and the power plants framing the sunset. "The only problem is the weather," he says. I look up at the clouds. They are a deep purple, "That can't be good." I give him a hug, "Congratulations, Dad."

I'm trying to finish a deadline so I can leave the office on time. I have a date with a Julie, a girl who used to work at the computer center. I send a file using the pneumatic tube and shower in my cubicle. Everyone has left for the day except a co-worker, who continues to tell me about his plans for the weekend—I continue to lather my body with soap.

Julie arrives at the new house. My mother doesn't like her for some reason. We leave the family room to watch television in the kitchen. I'm having trouble breathing when someone knocks at the front door. We can see her silhouette standing on the porch.

~ 65 ~

Waiting. Pacing. The curve of the world always a step ahead as I consider my walk. Amazing how green and blue compliment each other so well. Sitting. Standing. Watching the day pass me by. Impatient. Anxious. Where is she?

~ 66 ~

Our last kiss goodnight and the world seems somehow smaller. With her eyes closed, she hugs, her head digging into my chest, her tears seeping through my shirt. I walk down her driveway, deliberately—the stars, the moon—I wish I could fly. The sky looks like the ocean—I wish I could swim. The air is cold enough to watch myself breathe. I feel the night in my lungs. I feel alive. The sound of a harmonica and another slow drive through Carbon Canyon, slow because my headlights never shine past the turns. A long line of businessmen, wearing business suits, run a trail alongside the road. A deer stops in front of me.

~ 67 ~

A horse. Everyone is trying to kill this beautiful horse. They want to use his skin, his muscles and his bones. I just want to run my fingers through his mane. I try to help, but I don't know how to ride a horse. I feel so inadequate.

~ 68 ~

I stand on the roof of a high-rise building. The view is breathtaking. The wind settles at my feet and it feels as though it is lifting me, like I could step out onto the air breaking before me. "Falling isn't easy," Brett says while waiting. He is next in line.

~ **69** ~

My friend's father is on the phone. I'm not quite sure why he called. I guess, recently, he suffered another bout with cancer. He's sharing a story about his neighbor. I listen, attentively, but I still worry about his health.

~ 70 ~

My brother parked his car in a lot filled with traffic pylons, safety cones, and caution tape. The block was under construction and waist-high weeds, grass, and brush had broken through the asphalt. Clouds were resting heavy on skyscraper roofs and spilling rain like waterfalls down building sides. My brother and I walked to a filling station that was hosting a fashion show. I was nervous because Jenica, who recently separated from her husband, started working at one of the shops in the neighboring strip mall. The runway presentation was broadcast on a tiny transistor television sitting near the convenience store register. It was difficult to see what was happening, but we could hear applause; we exited stage left.

~ 71 ~

I sit at my computer in my college dorm. My dad enters the room. He seems irritable. A couple follow close behind, they embrace one another, crying. As they sit at the foot of my bed my dad closes the door. He looks over at me, disappointed.

~ 72 ~

Downtown Chicago. We're visiting my grandmother and the weather is perfect. A stiff breeze is holding clouds back over Lake Michigan as we walk along Columbus Drive in Grant Park. My mother asks my father if we should stay, "Of course, we've been wanting to do this as a family for years." My brother and I are kicking a rock back and forth as we walk, it skips up past my father. I haven't seen my father this happy in a while, he kicks the rock back to me and I pass it over to Ryan. My grandmother sits on the Buckingham Fountain's marble edge as my parents debate our next stop. My brother and I are watching tourists when the fountain begins to overflow, completely drenching my grandmother and leaving us ankle deep in water. Her once fluffy, permed, hair is now sopping wet and flat. She seems smaller—more frail, more delicate. I grab a towel to dry her hair, "Want to leave?" I don't want her to catch a cold on this autumn afternoon. "Let's check out the circus tent," my father cheers enthusiastically. As my father leads our family along the landscaped grounds, I fall behind, staring at storefronts and carnival booths. A gentleman behind us is asking every girl he passes if they'd want to be his Valentine. I think he's homeless and stole his flowers from a nearby garden. A woman grabs his hand, asking him to go home, "Get some sleep," she says, "You've been here for three days straight."

~ 73 ~

We are sitting in the top row of an immense concert hall. The stage is nowhere to be found. Everyone is looking in the same direction, but I know they can't see anything either. I grab Ebony's hand and we leave. The aisle is never-ending as we politely pass long legs and anxious knees. Somehow, I lose her and trace my steps back through the audience to find her.

~ 74 ~

Clean. Vacuum. Dust corners. Straighten frames. I don't even recognize the pictures on these walls. My brother and I want a new fence for the front yard—a white picket fence made of redwood. We want something that will remind us of summer. The neighbors are watching us. I feel uneasy and keep my head down as I work on the house...Teresa on my mind.

~ 75 ~

Fourth grade. Hopkinson Elementary. My team consists of the hopeless and the useless—the losers left along the sideline. We are in the final seconds of the game and everyone is exhausted as we huddle together, "We don't stand a chance," I state, smiling at my fellow classmates, "I like these odds." We break and run to our positions. Like a bull preparing to charge, Joey digs his cleats into the grass near the net. Stretching his hamstrings and quadriceps, Matt plants his foot for perfection, anticipating a shot at goal. I stand at the corner—ready. The field looks perfect, the weather is perfect, the referee blows his whistle. I step back before stepping forward.

~ 76 ~

Wildflower. My desert sun, I dance alone. I wish my tuxedo fit better around the shoulders and longer along the arms. My poorly shined shoes kick up dust with my rusty two-step—uncoordinated and awkward. I'm holding onto her much too tightly because I am nervous. She always said *nothing is forever*, and that they would find me. But, I am ready, and I will finish this dry lake waltz, our song haunting the hills.

A feather falls from the sky.

~ 77 ~

A heavy fog rolls with my wandering step. Aimlessly, I follow fading street lamps that polka dot the distance—and this road is long. Meet me in the gray. I will wait for your headlights.

31

~ 78 ~

The ocean is dark and dense like bunker fuel. Old wharfies sit along the coast drinking sea salt Guinness. Nathan and I watch for whales, but I'm always looking over my shoulder, scared of something. The world sways as the water rises and a small dolphin says hello.

Back at a motel, we pack for our drive north. A cleaning lady enters the room. She's stunning with smooth black hair that waves with her stride. She doesn't speak English very well, but she sure smiles a lot. We call her Lily. "I don't want to leave anymore, Nathan." He sits on his luggage so he can pull the zipper closed. "I just want to hold Lily, just wrap around her waist and never let go of those hips."

Nathan is on the phone, nodding his head while listening to a friend. With his hand over the transmitter he gets my attention, "It doesn't look like he'll make it tonight." He says goodbye and hangs up the phone. "I need some air," Nathan steps outside as another maid enters the room. The name on her tag reads *Atlanta*. I hide our wallets in the same drawer that conceals the Gideon Bible. Lily is on the bed slowly removing her clothes. I walk toward her with two five-dollar bills as Atlanta vacuums. I take my shirt off as the phone rings. Atlanta answers, as if expecting the call, and she talks for a while. Lily and I pull playfully at the sheets and start kissing when Atlanta gives me the handset, "It's for you." The lady on the other end of the line is whispering, "Kevin. The room is wired." I hang up.

~ 79 ~

I am sitting on an arched stone seating area designed around the campus courtyard. My friends have scattered and gathered into little groups. I feel as if they are talking about me. Someone I remember from freshman year rolls up to me in a hospital wheelchair—he stands up and collapses its frame. He is much more talkative than I remember him.

~ 80 ~

Dodger Stadium is packed past capacity as people pile on top of one another, standing on shoulders, hoping to get a better view of the game.

As we leave in a city shuttle, students shout at our van. The neighborhood surrounding Chavez Ravine is under construction; scaffolding can be seen all along the San Gabriel Mountains. It looks like they are building more stadiums.

Security routes traffic through Elysian Park. A local radio station is playing soul classics—Bloodstone, "Natural High," then "For the Love of You," by The Isley Brothers. I sing quietly to myself as we take a detour.

~ 81 ~

I try to type the day when I notice my Underwood is cleaner than usual. My mother must have taken a cloth to the keys. Each letter I strike smashes the stiff typebar into the platen causing a spark—parts shatter into pieces, words no longer print on my paper. I pull out the sheet and ink drips everywhere. I run my story through the roller one last time and hold it up to the light, "That's curious."

~ 82 ~

Walking down a dirt road, we debate the quality of temporary tattoos. Every time a car drives by we stop and stand off to the shoulder. Inflation has played a big role in the sale of body art.

~ 83 ~

I wonder why Amber has a friend at her side at all times. And why this friend, despite how I feel for Amber, is always flirting with me. I steal some seconds alone with Amber as we run down an irrigation tunnel that leads to the other side of town—laughing, out of breath, playfully hiding in shadows while dragging steel rods along the corrugated piping channel. We find our way back to Casey's, the diner where Amber, her friend, and I work—the diner below the apartment where Amber, her friend, and I live.

~ 84 ~

Another party and I'm still looking for a way out. A few friends from film school make it a point to interrupt the conversations I start. I find another bar in another room. Jason stands behind a table wearing a white suit with coattails, "This reunion is like every other god damned reunion," he says, "Only the ties and the music are different." I agree and walk into another room. I hope a fight will break out—to expedite the process, I instigate. A push here, a punch there, and then Ken shows up and he looks stunning, handsome. I run toward him and jump onto his chest, climbing over his shoulders. He is much larger than I remember, at least 12 inches taller and 12 pounds heavier. His cheeks are turning pink. Ken was always shy.

~ 85 ~

Sitting in a wooden windsor with my feet up on the porch railing smoking a cigarette. I don't smoke, but the sunset on the farm is beautiful.

~ 86 ~

Laying poolside in swim trunks and a corduroy sport coat—
preparing to introduce summer to autumn. Nick rubs tanning
oil on my legs and talks about romantic comedies of the
nineties as the girls who just moved into an apartment behind
mine jump into the deep end. We follow. The water is warm
and thin and it feels like we're floating. I pull my goggles back
down over my eyes, button the flaps of my aviator hat, and
stare at the stars.

~ 87 ~

As the assistant director on the set, it is my responsibility to manage the cast and crew, however I am furious with our prop master because he's letting everyone eat the corn tortillas we need for the next scene.

~ 88 ~

Josh and I are riding bikes inland from the beach in Huntington. There just isn't enough room on the sidewalks as people walk in the streets. We stop at a shirt and shoe shop, which used to be a gas station. The owner of the retailer recently dropped out of community college to take a chance on an idea. The shirts on display were so small they wouldn't even fit on a finger, but he claimed the novelty of this concept helped sell more fabric, "Which is where the money is." He was only selling one pair of shoes—the shoes he was wearing on his own two feet. They were limited edition Air Jordans circa 1989. "If I walk cool and I talk cool, people will want my shoes. I'll even autograph the sole, but that costs extra." I used to have those shoes when I was younger, and I have to admit, he did walk cool and he did talk cool and I did want to buy them, but they weren't my size. I purchased some fabric instead.

Outside we were preparing for a photo-shoot with Colin and Chris. Colin is our staff photographer and Chris is the talent. Chris is a lot older than I had anticipated, somewhere in his seventies, but everyone seems to get along just fine. A few girls are hanging around craft services, which consists of watermelon and a bowl of butter with small serving spoons. The girls seem nice. I've run out of business cards so I tear off sheets from my notepad, folding the paper until they're the size of business cards—they can't tell the difference. I walk to my car because I've run out of paper and find Shaun swinging a golf club hitting golf balls over the highway into the hills. His golf club is broken. We hug. I haven't seen him since high school basketball. Now everyone in Huntington is swinging a golf club hitting golf balls over the highway into the hills.

~ 89 ~

I am showering in the Grand Hotel lobby. I notice Nick and
his wife, Josh and his wife, and Morgan and his wife, checking
in at the front desk. I lather myself up with soap hoping they
won't see me. Someone forgot a camera on the tile floor near
my feet. I move it so it won't get wet.

~ 90 ~

I am listening to a message on my phone as I enter the gym. A girl is yelling on my machine and I'm nervous everyone can hear. I walk through the basketball game, past the ellipticals, toward the machine weight circuit. I set my equipment bag down by the shoulder press as a girl across from me on the seated leg extension motions that she can help. I shrug it off with a submissive smile, as if to say there is nothing I can do. I'm not sure why I didn't just hang up.

I am desperately trying to find a bathroom. Club members sit at their lockers changing into leisure suits. I desperately want to fit in and jump into conversation with a gentleman talking about business economics—I agree with his opinions to help build trust. Another guy is ordering pizza, he was put on hold, but tells us how the lady on the line told him to "Nine it," to which I start a string of jokes using "Nine it" as the punchline. Everyone is laughing, even though, we know, she meant he owed nine dollars.

~ 91 ~

We're exchanging gifts with our relatives at a family picnic. Everybody has a wrapped box in their lap, but nobody is paying attention to anything.

A super-sized parking structure has cars stacked in vertical piles and organized in color-coordinated rows.

Stressed shoppers rush for sales and sales and sales with bags and bags and bags—climbing shelf-mountains. Carelessly, I roll on heel skates with an unassuming smile, but trip over a crack in the linoleum floor. I think it's funny.

~ 92 ~

It's four in the morning; Hunter and I lean against his Pontiac Sunbird while filling its tank with gas. He's on a house phone with a cord that stretches down the highway. He's leaving a message for his girlfriend when I notice a faraway light in the field. Maybe it's another gas station.

~ 93 ~

Walking from one room to another in an old plantation-style house on prairie Badlands. I can't be certain whether I'm guest or family. Everyone is cleaning around the house, but their work is worthless as the Dakota winds simply replace all displaced dust. I sit on a gooseneck armchair near a window to admire the long field and low sky—beige and blue. I notice two black & white, framed portraits on the wall—one of a mother and the other of a father. I start to cry and leave to wander the halls. My friend Magda is stretching on the floor in an empty room; I have always been intrigued by her. She has magnificent cheekbones and her smile is magnetic. With my hands, I climb up a wall to the second floor. Spiders, coming out from foundation cracks, crawl all over my hands and up my arms, causing me to fall—abruptly. I remove my clothes, shaking out my shirt and pants, frantically brushing off spiders. Magda shouts from the other room, "Turn off the phone!"

~ 94 ~

Joey, a friend of mine from the neighborhood, planned a party at his house. He invited the entire block. My plan was to arrive late and leave early, but my plan changed when I met Dee. She was sitting on the couch watching basketball playoffs. With one hand holding the remote, she switched stations every commercial break to keep up on all the scores of the night. Her other hand switched between a dry martini and cold pizza. Her ex-husband, Alex, was into war-themed board games and was playing Risk in the kitchen. Dee and I kissed our way to the bedroom and wrestled off our clothes.

Dee and I were back on the couch watching game and player highlights. Brushing her hair to the side, I kissed her on the forehead—then, I ran. I ran out the front door into the cold night, down the street toward my parent's house—my heavy breathing forms clouds of condensation, my heavy heart-beating punches my ribs. I was scared, deeply scared.

I woke up late and my brother and I hopped into his car to drive back to Joey's house. I had forgotten my wallet and my keys. Everyone from the party was still sleeping. Dee was talking to a peace officer who was writing everything she was saying. Alex was sitting on the couch staring at his feet. He seemed embarrassed. Joey came into the room and greeted me with a huge hug. He held me so tight I couldn't breathe.

I found my wallet and my keys and my brother and I got back into his car. He was driving recklessly on our way home—running over curbs and ramming into cars. I was still trying to figure out what happened between Dee and Alex. As my brother merged onto the freeway I hopped out of the car.

~ 95 ~

In the back seat of our van—my father driving, my mother beside him—climbing a steep and narrow road that wraps tightly around a slender mountain up through the clouds. I'm afraid to look out my window because heights frighten me. We can't seem to find our terminal, but our flight isn't scheduled to leave until later tonight. Large diesel machines manage the airport as aliens tour the galaxies. My parents haven't told me what planet we're visiting.

~ 96 ~

We're in the living room watching an old teammate play the comedic sidekick to a robot scientist in some new romantic comedy entitled "Naturally." The robot, cleverly named Rob, is made of rusted scrap metal and towers over skyscrapers, but he's sensitive, that's why it's funny. I think that's why America tunes in every week to see what will happen next. In this episode, Rob plans to take over the world, despite his friendly disposition. America loves irony.

~ 97 ~

The steering wheel melts in my hands as I turn, the tires spin off in different directions, and my car crashes into everything in its path—curb, streetlight, car, house. I am angered and frustrated. I can see my parents walking on the sidewalk in my rearview mirror. I try again. Crash! What is wrong with me? Why can't I turn? Crash! Jasper crosses the street and knocks on my window. He is the last person I'd want to see right now. I reluctantly roll down the glass. "You know," he says, "the mountains are the best place to see clearly." He winks and walks away. I feel congested. My car is filthy. I start picking up some trash and spill dirt in my chocolate milk. This upsets me.

~ 98 ~

Watching television with my parents. We're finishing a special on traveling. A group of girls documented their vacation into the forest—climbing up treetops, backpacking through woods, skinny-dipping in rivers. A masculine voice-over narrates a thematic coming-of-age story juxtaposed with an emotional string orchestra score. The message: reform. Let's start from the beginning.

~ 99 ~

A city-side statesman stands on the corner of a downtown street slum. He holds a sign that reads, "Help yourself!" The area is run by gangs and I run with a crew of three. A young gentleman being chased by a convict swinging a wooden bat runs past us. "Susceptibility," my friend says, "Today, lawless. Tomorrow, they'll turn us all into lambs."

The three of us walk into a nearby park with lambs grazing in the grass. There doesn't seem to be enough grass for everyone. We enter the tennis courts and lock the gate behind us. We climb up the 10 foot chain-linked fence and can see the entire county, "It's beautiful," I mutter under my breath, when I am suddenly pulled down from the steel-top tubing.

We are soaring together when she says, "I am neither lamb nor wolf."

~ 100 ~

I notice her leave a classroom before the bell rings. I follow her down the university hall. It is the middle of winter and I wasn't prepared for Boston weather. She places her books in her locker and walks outside into the courtyard. I'll need a parka.

~ 100 ~

~ 101 ~

It's a hot August day and I'm working in my front yard garden. The sky is cloudless, but splashes of water sprinkle over me. Blocking the sun with my hand I give it a second look and notice an invisible fighter plane hovering over my neighborhood. We hear planes all the time because we live near a military base, but not only was this plane invisible, it was silent. The pilot lands in the street and opens his cockpit door, "There's something you need to see," he hands me a tabloid magazine, "we need to take care of this."

In a Fiat 850 with a short and stout Italian man sporting a long mustache that rolls in spring-like circles around his cheeks. He's sweating through his clothes and through his car seat, nervously chatting about paparazzo.

CUT TO:

Amy and some actor walk down a back lot street in some New York style Hollywood scene. Her Mississippi Delta accent is terrible, "You have to admit there is a kind of likeness about us," pointing at a picture printed in the gossip column of my tabloid magazine beneath the headline, "Star-crossed". A studio squad car speeds past, followed by an ambulance and a fire engine—all with sirens screaming. Amy drops the magazine—wind blowing pages past photos of the two of us. The entire set is on fire; all of the building facades are crumbling to the ground. The Fiat 850 is upside down and engulfed in flames. The set looks as though a war had interrupted their shooting schedule. Amy is shocked to see me across the street, working in my front yard garden. She runs over to me, crying, "What happened?" I look up at her, blood dripping from my mouth, my left eye swollen shut with bruises changing the landscape of my face, "We need to do something about those pictures."

~ 102 ~

The cove is covered with small shed-roofed, exposed wood homes that were built into the recesses of the coast. Greg and I walk barefoot along a creek drinking wine from Dixie cups— no computers, no phones, no deadlines. His advice is comforting and he offers to share a list of contacts with Josh when we return to the mainland. Sean arrives on a steam engine tugboat that is pulling a log raft. He is beyond drunk and convinced that books are killing the environment, "Recycle your paperbacks! Read trees!"

I would visit the island again years after they built a skatepark along the shore. Commercial sponsors picture prominently along the horizon and the sands had been divided evenly among Silicon Valley dot-coms. My brother was asleep on the couch, Jenica was arriving later, and I was walking barefoot along a creek drinking wine from a Dixie cup talking to a documentarian with a large studio camera over his shoulder. I feel fake. I don't want to talk anymore.

~ 103 ~

The broadcast is interrupted with a special bulletin. A government official leaked news of a political summit in the hills of Burke, Vermont. They're calling it a gathering of minds—activists, engineers, mathematicians, physicists—idealists uniting to prevent global chaos caused by religious wars. The anchor reads off a transcript, "This is a world problem that requires prompt and decisive action." The military has begun to withdraw troops from other regions to protect and patrol our borders, national banks have ceased all financial transactions including withdrawals, and international delegates and officials were immediately discharged of their duties. Patriotism. Patriotism was the answer. Patriotism was a fundamental solution, a policy that could build back our economy and restore a common faith, a simple faith in our people.

I was walking to a local market and traffic was riotous. People were crowding the streets in celebration. Today marked the year North Axis seceded from South Axis—a date marked by an ecosystem failure that spread over half the continents making 60 percent of dry land uninhabitable. I just needed bread to make a sandwich and I didn't want to participate in any party that I wasn't invited to. You see, everything changed after Fourth War. New law overturned longstanding citizenship rulings and it was unanimously decided to allow anyone to root anywhere, which is why I feel like a foreigner on my own soil. On a television in the local deli, a news reporter was in the middle of the madness. He was reporting that crime had decreased dramatically since the institution of "Ever-Search", a surveillance program produced by contracted policing. Scrolling across the bottom of the television screen was a status ticker informing citizens of current criminals and suspicious activity. With my half baguette in hand I noticed my name scroll across the monitor. I know the system has its flaws, but my name had been erased before the rebellion. I never approved of "Ever-Search" and tactically fell off this corporate grid. My name scrolled along the screen again. Something is wrong. I turn to start back for home when a dirty bomb explodes in the middle of downtown. Then a building implodes and crumbles to the ground with fires igniting around the city—bombs, missiles, grenades—familiar sounds of scatter and screaming. I help a teenager in a wheelchair out of the street and away from the chaos. He looks up at me, strangely. Something is definitely wrong. He wheels down the street while pulling an automatic rifle from inside the sidearm of his chair—shooting at a safety zeppelin that was surveying the scene. The blimp ignites into a hydrogen fire cloud and falls from the sky burning the entire block. Before I have a chance to react the kid has started running down a back alley. I chase after him.

~ 104 ~

We're shooting empty beer cans from the living room into the kitchen garbage. Rollie is at the edge of the carpet with his toes on the tile floor. He shoots, but Travis swats his can into a wall, beer bursting everywhere. The can wasn't empty. Travis is acting strange, laughing when nothing is funny, seemingly depressed but seemingly smiling. Josh is on the couch watching television, waiting his turn. I am sitting on the counter enjoying every minute. Chris arrives to tell us that he no longer plays sports, "I've taken my talent to the stage." We later learn that Chris only books dramatic athletic roles. He sings for us, but nobody seems impressed, but that doesn't mean we don't consider him a friend.

~ 105 ~

Standing backstage for another reality television show recording. They shoot everything on a set but use a live studio audience. My brother feels the need to be on camera and sticks his head out from around the stage curtain. I am trying to get the attention of a girl sitting in a make-up chair when my brother starts giggling hysterically, "Live television, Ladies and Gentleman."

~ 106 ~

Brittany, Catherine, and I bike through a half-built shopping center in the Great Basin Desert near Black Rock. Somehow, we effortlessly ride without ever having to pedal or turn, flying over huge holes in the ground and through unfinished walls of stick and box frames that have been covered with blue poly tarps that blow in the wind. We lock our bikes to the stairwell of my apartment and walk toward a lake-size dirt puddle. For some reason Brittany believes that this body of water is bottomless, and she wants to swim to the other side.

~ 107 ~

While waiting to purchase tickets with Wendy, I notice this incessant line is full of homeless veterans. Seats have been removed from the concert hall balcony to accommodate overflow from the local shelter. Over the years, Oakland has grown dirtier and dustier, and is almost unrecognizable. The city looks like a wasteland with trash piles collecting high around houses creating home-hills with holes cut into each roof for entry. We reach the front of the line where two bouncers stand with their arms crossed. I want to pay but forgot my wallet. Wendy reaches into her purse and inconspicuously pulls out a twenty-dollar bill. The girl behind the counter gives Wendy a look then gives her directions to the performance. We drive through the countryside past shelterbelt trees that block the wind from passing anything from Oakland into the greenlands. As we pass the cityline, Wendy rolls down our windows, and I stare up at the still moving sky that gradually changes from gray to blue.

~ 108 ~

An escalator leads to a cliff at the end of the world. It's a slow and long goodbye—hugging, reminiscing, laughing. Kids stand near the edge, curiously looking down into the canyon, optimistically looking out over the horizon. A heavy sun hangs over our heads, a half moon at its side, as children play on this steady-moving stair. Up ahead, two kids tumble over the ledge, but nobody is paying attention. Another kid, with his pant leg caught in the step tread is pulled into the gulley. I look around, hoping someone will help, as a third, fourth, and fifth kid dies. One after another they fall, laughing along the way, I don't hear any screams, I don't hear anyone crying.

~ 109 ~

Jack opened a new restaurant on the peninsula so I took a subway to the headland. My date was meeting me there, but I was already disappointed and despondent. I sat in the far corner of the room to avoid conversation. When my date arrived, we are already arguing. I stood up and walked toward Jack and his wife. While we talked, a guy placed a sticker on my drinking glass, which was still in my hand. This angered me. I went back to my seat where my date, with her arms crossed, refused to talk. A waitress took my order, I asked for steak. She gave me a look before walking back into the kitchen. The music was getting louder when a server brought two uncooked steaks to our table. I didn't like the look on the server's face so I turned the plate over onto his head. The music stopped and everyone turned toward me. My date walked out the front door, embarrassed. I threw my drinking glass, still with a sticker, onto the floor and stormed through the party—intentionally bumping into people and knocking things over. I took someone's drink out of their hand and slowly poured it onto the table.

It was cold outside. The street was damp and quiet. I dug my hands deep into my pockets, shrugged my shoulders, lowered my head, and I walked back to the subway.

~ 110 ~

Kids play stickball between rail lines in the Union Stock Yards as several suits question union workers who live west of the packing plants. Something happened last night in Chicago between the Irish and the Germans, but nobody is talking.

~ 111 ~

Tracy pulls my arm, hangs on my shoulder—she is always trying to get my attention—as a girl across the room flirts from a distance with longing glances. Occasionally, this girl will walk past me, brushing up against me, her perfume leaving a trail I want to follow, but Tracy grabs my hand and holds me back, refusing to let go.

~ 112 ~

I'm visiting Michelle's house. She's dating someone new. I'm trying to convince her family that he will never be what Michelle needs. I prepare a speech to present in front of everyone, including the new guy. I'm standing at the front door, my hands trembling, it's obvious I still love her, "You should be doing great things, Michelle. You are greater than this. Don't settle, not for this, not for anything." I pause for a moment. 'I still believe in you.' I close the door behind me. I wonder what they are talking about as I walk across the street. I hope she'll come running out that door chasing after me.

~ 113 ~

The San Diego coast, at the deep-water port landing facility near the Mexico border, is crowded with tourists anticipating the return of Space Shuttle Ceres. This test study was the first in the agronomy program, which sent sharecroppers into outer space. Their objective was to explore the mind-farming theory in alternative atmospheres.

~ 114 ~

My system is failing as I float through distant galaxies. My suit has a hole in it and I am slowly losing oxygen. I am tired and I want to close my eyes, but the sights are just too beautiful.

~ 115 ~

Tent cities form desert communes outside a massive concrete dome. Families gather near campfires singing songs and sharing stories. A few friends battle and brawl, grappling with one another for rank and status. I wander the shadows of our dimly lit refuge and stare into the distant darkness. Nobody knows what waits for us beyond our sanctuary; we might be the only survivors. I leave tonight as everyone sleeps.

~ 116 ~

I stand behind an M1919 Browning machine gun mounted to the back of a military jeep that barrels through downtown. The financial district was burnt to the ground and the abandoned buildings around it, if they haven't already been demolished, are used as criminal hideouts and lookout posts. My eyes watch the skyline as we enter an underground parking structure.

~ 117 ~

The phone rings, "Hello?" A soft whisper breathes through the line, "Please help me, please..." she is short of breath and I can't understand what she's saying. "Hello. My name is Raquel. We're selling magazine subscriptions..." I interrupt her, "I'm sorry, just now, before, I couldn't quite understand what you were saying." She ignores me. "Hello. My name is Raquel. We're selling magazine subscriptions." "I'm sorry. I'm not interested." I hang up the phone, a little confused.

Later that night, when talking to my mother, she tells me of a similar situation she had several months back. After some research she found out these girls on the other end were being held captive. Human trafficking. They were kidnapped from other countries and forced to perform services like...telemarketing. I guess one time, my mother tried to help a girl and left money in an airport locker, but she never knew what happened after that.

~ 118 ~

Sitting in a tub filled with soap bubbles, water spilling over the side and splashing onto the tile floor. I hear a buzz whipping around the bathroom. It gets louder and closer to my ear and then it stops. A hornet is sitting near my feet. I can see him breathing, his little legs slipping and sliding on the wet porcelain. I am scared and I don't move, but I know I must get rid of him. He must die. He must die before he kills me. I kick my legs, creating waves of water that crash over him, and he falls into the bath with me. I can see him trying to swim, but he is sinking. I dump palms of water over him, water splashing everywhere. He is slowly dying, his legs slowly kicking as he drifts toward the bottom of the tub. I can still see him breathing, so I grab my coffee mug and plunge it into the water, pressing its side into his little body, cracking, crunching, crushing this little hornet between porcelain tub and porcelain mug until he is dead. I still hear buzzing.

~ 119 ~

Spanish Harlem on my mind—Dominican, Salvadoran and Mexican Manhattan. Madness. Abandon. Tow sack packed with a world in waiting—check-in, baggage, customs, and boarding gate. Transportation security watches a fire burn along the airport apron and spread onto the runway. My ticket says Chicago, but I don't think I will ever find home again.

~ 120 ~

Summer seasoned with orange scented sun. Her father unwinds in a rocker recliner near the backroom screen door, college golf on television; his basset sleeps beside him. I knock before entering. He gets up to greet me, "The kids are out back. Did you bring your trunks?" Outside, everyone sits in a small poly pool. I recognize a friend on a toy slide drinking wine coolers. I don't fit in, but I tell myself I should write a story about this. For some reason I start to cry and the hound is licking the palm of my hand.

~ 121 ~

Summer camp and we're finger-painting with instant pudding. A boy is drawing on my shoes when a girl falls into a tub of chocolate-vanilla swirl. I am unhappy and jump a wall into a neighbor's yard. I fly, pulling myself forward from tree to tree, branch to branch. Dads are coming home from work and moms are cooking in the kitchen. The sun sets.

~ 122 ~

The grounds-crew harvest spring lemons in the outfield as the Los Angeles Dodgers finish batting practice. The team looks saintly in their home uniforms. In the bullpen, Orel Hershiser is sick with a thermometer in his mouth and an ice pack on his head. Kirk Gibson is injured and pulls a push reel lawn mower across the grass near the dugout. I am alone in the stands when I see a flash from a camera.

A motorhome drives along the coast and across a bridge before arriving at an abandoned carnival.

~ 123 ~

I think that's her. It has to be her. Those beautiful eyes. Those beautiful little round eyes. They were bright blue. I remember them being bright blue. Her teeth were sharp, straight; they didn't seem to fit her crooked smile. That smile. But it was those eyes that got me into trouble in the first place. I'm packing, or cleaning, and I'm carrying a suitcase and wearing a tie and a sport coat with elbow holes. I think the jacket was my father's. She says something to me then smiles. Boy did she ever have a beautiful smile. I didn't quite catch what she said. I took off my hat, straightened my hair once over, she smiled and said it again, "You can go, I really won't need your help," and it was just like that, she smiled her smile, a sincere smile, a smile of understanding. It was the kind of smile that told you it was over. I placed my hat back on my head, tucking my hair over my ears and into the band of the derby. She was fixing my tie when I placed my hand over hers. It felt good touching her. I would truly miss that, that and her smile, and those eyes. I kissed her on the forehead and said goodbye. I think it was her, but I'm not quite sure. Either way, it felt nice—it felt familiar.

~ 124 ~

When I return home, I want a new truck because my old Ford is rundown and has trouble turning corners. The paint falls off in chips as I ride the interstate. The engine turns over as if it were sick and aching, especially when my morning drive happens before sunrise. My parents accompany me to the local used lot where we know a salesman who could help us out. I just want something to get me from point A to point B. And then it dawned on me—I just got a new car. I got a new car last week. What ever happened to that car? It was a new wagon with air-conditioning and power steering. I asked my mom, "Didn't we just get a new car?" She put her hand on my forehead, concerned, as if I was ill, like something was wrong. "Remember the baby blue wagon?" My dad walked back to us after a long conversation with the dealer, "I think I can get us a good deal on another pick-up," he looked at my mother, then over to me, "What's wrong?" My mother explained everything and we spent the rest of the day trying to find the wagon.

My friend Mike picks me up. He needs new shoes. We drove around town stopping at local strip malls in search of the perfect fit. He never found it. As we drove home we were stopped at a roadblock. The police set up a barricade and investigators were wrapping a corner house with caution tape. I guess the old man who lived in that old craftsman had been murdered. He had lived in that house since the 1930s, well before my family moved into the neighborhood. His dog was still in the yard barking. They decided it would be appropriate to play Lisa's speech from her father's funeral. Her father had died earlier that month, and her father was friends with the old man, and the old man didn't have any family, just his dog. Everyone stood along the curb with their hats off and their heads down. In the recording, Lisa spoke of loss and regret, and it really moved everyone on the block.

~ 125 ~

Back at the hotel a businesswoman was flirting with me. We would kiss a little then I'd walk to the other side of the room until the moment presented itself. Then we'd kiss again and maybe remove some clothing. I was continuously trying to create mood, changing songs, adjusting the lighting by playing with the blinds. She was growing impatient, but she was beautiful. She had dark brown hair and thick red lipstick. I think she was Hispanic.

Then I went dancing at a club on Main Street. A local jazz quartet played every Sunday night and the building was full of energy. Everyone was drinking in celebration of my birthday or some accomplishment from earlier that day, and I helped a man fix his antique roll-top desk before going home. He said it was for his kid.

~ 126 ~

I'm in the middle seat of an old family van. Behind the wheel sits Largo, an overweight half-wit. His half-buttoned neon Hawaiian shirt is obnoxious. It nauseates me. He's driving me to a meeting downtown. I have everything with me—my films, my photos, my books, my journals—everything. As we approach a bridge, he slows down. The view is breathtaking. A river wraps around mountains that break into the sky. A train slowly passes on the road-rail with cargo. Dust and debris and desiccated pieces of wood tremble as the steel wheels of the locomotive turn. I never liked bridges, "There must be another way, possibly an alternate route?" I warn Largo to slow, to stop, when the bridge suddenly collapses, and we crash straight into the water below. Everything—my films, my photos, my books, my journals—sinking to the bottom. I manage to save only my Smith Corona typewriter and swim to the top, kicking and screaming, but it is useless. Everything I ever created is gone. Largo just didn't get it. He was staring at me, blank eyed with a goofy grin. An art class was painting near an underpass. A girl with short hair was bothered by my rage. I began directing my anger toward her—my voice cracking with frustration. She didn't get it. I went to a friend's movie release later that night and tried to blame him. A guest in line was singing songs to his girlfriend. He was singing the wrong lyrics. I was furious. He didn't get it.

~ 127 ~

The gymnasium is crowded with players practicing, preparing for the first round of tournament play. I recognize a few familiar faces, teammates from junior league, from high school, but I am sick, and won't be able to participate. I'm walking around talking to everyone. I look confident and content. I am chosen as the team captain and get first pick. I survey the room before selecting Matt— mainly due to his height—who is warming up on the other side of the court. My second pick is Brian because he hustles. Josh challenges me to a quick game of one-on-one and I oblige, still wearing street clothes. While dribbling around him his hand gets stuck inside my shirt, and he pulls me away from the hoop. I scream and collapse to the floor. There is a sudden sharp pain on my left hip-bone. I pull my shirt up to find a deep gash in my side, which is bleeding profusely. Josh looks at his hand and his wedding band is covered in blood. The diamond of his ring clean cut my skin leaving my bone exposed. I closed my eyes in agony as everyone continued shooting baskets.

~ 128 ~

It was a soaring building, a thin pile of bricks that tore through the clouds. They say it was the first high-rise structure built on the west coast. We were waiting for the maintenance elevator, Tom and I, and some lady holding her bag against her chest. When it arrived, the doors hesitated to open. I pulled the gate for the lady and politely let her enter first, "You go on ahead without us. We'll wait." Tom and I would wait until the elevator went up to the next floor. We walked through an empty space behind the door that led to a hidden hallway behind the elevator shaft. We were hanging out with friends at a cigar lounge with a view of the ocean. There was hardly enough room to stand and we climbed from group to group. Even though people surrounded us, I was getting lonely.

Driving along the coast, listening to the reluctant beach breeze, looking for somebody.

~ 129 ~

I invited friends to my house—and then, I opened a closet in the hallway. My rifle was leaning up against the wall. Tying the strap over my shoulder I tucked the butt of the gun under my right arm. Slowly and selectively I started shooting. Repercussions? Not a worry on my mind. It was almost playful, like finding fawn in the forest. Nobody seemed startled or scared. They would just look at me, anticipating bullets, but the gun wasn't working. Maybe I just didn't know how to accurately aim. I pumped the Winchester hoping that might help, but I continued shooting mere reminders. I walked through the house, room after room, innocently trying to shoot anything in sight before my parents came home. Now, I've had this dream before. I almost know how it ends. One of the girls at the party will manage to kill me before I can escape. So, I calmly handed over my gun and turned around. I could feel her figuring out how to use the gun. While I tried to fly I could sense her questioning if she should retaliate for my behavior. I got nervous and desperate to get away. I jumped the fence in our backyard and climbed a tree, branch by branch, in an attempt to reach the sky. I could feel her aiming the rifle at my back—my arm stretched up for a cloud as I closed my eyes.

~ 130 ~

Everyone was back in town for the holidays. Without any planning, everyone somehow found his or her way to Joey's house. It was just like the old days, his parents were gone, the fridge was filled with drinks, and every clique clicked into different rooms. I was alone, wandering from one area to another. You see, the thing is, I was friends with all of them, but never really fit in. Oh, and I wasn't drinking, which came across as if I thought I was better than everyone else. Travis was picking on me, as he always did. I asked him quietly and politely to not push me around, and he laughed. Girls were cooking something special in the kitchen when Patrick arrived. I hadn't seen Patrick in a while and I always looked up to him. We talked for a moment, then, I didn't see him again for the rest of the night. Maybe because I was hanging around the front door, debating—leave or stay, leave or stay. Brian was playing cards with a few other guys at the dining room table. I watched a quick hand then found myself in Leonard's apartment loft in Manhattan. He had a view of the entire city. We were talking about movies when a filmmaker friend of his joined in on the conversation. They were quoting films I had never seen. Two men were flying near his window on a hang glider performing acrobatic stunts and maneuvers. I was scared they would fall. My fear of heights was intensifying as the wind picked up. Leonard had something cooking in the kitchen and I really wanted to talk more about life and cinema. Driving home through the city I could hear sirens echoing off buildings. The streets were chaotic with everyone running in circles. Something was going on, but I continued driving.

~ 131 ~

Last night I dreamt of a flooding city. The ocean was overflowing and water spilled across the street and onto the sidewalk—houses were sinking. In an attempt to stay dry I ran up to the second story of a print shop. Everyone was laughing and drinking Guinness while watching waves wash up against the building walls. Nobody seemed to care.

When I woke up everything was fine. I drew back the blinds to look down the coastline and the water had reversed. I walked downstairs and out the front door where an old man using a shopping cart for balance greeted me, "Good day." I responded, politely, "How is everything?" He was heading toward an Irish Pub down the block, "They don't expect much from an old man…just stay out of trouble."

~ 132 ~

I found a family of four-inch deer living in my bedroom. I captured the father and forgot about him. I caught the mother and placed her inside my sweater pocket. The son was small and seemed lost. I watched him wander the floorboards along the wall. I tried to pick him up, but he would run away from me, scared, in search of a place to hide. I pinched his hind leg between my two fingers and placed him in the palm of my hand. He was soft and looked tired. He tilted his head up toward me and said he was having trouble finding food. I helped him catch a few spiders.

~ 133 ~

With dirt dusted boots dangling over the edge of an empty
cargo bed I sit still, silent, watching scenery change as we pass
through cities and states. The soft sound of Mourning Doves
sing as the sun rises, wings whistling as they take flight to
follow another smoke stack of yet another steam engine—
trains traveling through mountains, pushing, pulling freight—
forever along tracks that trace the contour of a subtle horizon.
Should be in California soon. Already missing Chicago.

Kevin Staniec

~ 134 ~

Floating distant in the deep pacific on an oak framed bed. My mattress and pillows are wrapped in plastic and I sleep with sheets, under stars, drifting toward the moon.

~ 135 ~

I imagine standing along the coast of Piaui dreaming blended cashew apple. It has been a while since I last saw Teresina. Alone I wander inland beneath low evergreen trees, walking backwards along my empty green city street. Catching mangos in the fabric of my shirt as they fall from the sky. I hum to myself as strangers happen on by.

~ 136 ~

I could hear my dad singing Christmas carols on the phone to relatives in Chicago. My mother was cooking breakfast before she opened my door to wake me up. "Have you seen it yet?" she asked while pulling up the shade. I rolled onto my side to look out the window. It was snowing. My father steps into the room wearing his robe and sipping a cup of coffee, "Did you notice that your mother decorated the tree in the front yard with ornaments?" A tractor slowly rolled by blowing snow across our lawn and down the street. "Who did this?" I asked. My mother said it was Craig and Dave our local real estate agents.

Later, we followed the holiday crowd and went to the movies. The theater resembled an airport. Concession stands were similar to baggage claims with rotating conveyor belts. Ticket booths had a security checkpoint with x-ray machines and metal detectors. Each terminal featured a different film as guests waiting in long lines walked down the passenger boarding bridge before entering the theater.

A stranger stopped to ask how I was doing. He seemed sure we had met prior to this introduction but I didn't recognize him at all. My friend Ian was coming up the escalator. We shared a quick hello. He was seeing a movie about a cheetah and a lemur.

I took a step outside for a breath of fresh air. The snow was still falling. The streets were busy with last minute shoppers. I love it when it snows in Orange County.

~ 137 ~

I woke to a feeling of vulnerability, feet tingling, hands shaking, my lungs gasping for air. My body was weak, as if a spirit had rushed my soul. My eyes wouldn't stop tearing, but I wasn't crying. My self—almost selfless—helpless.

My dream was interrupted by a moment: I was standing on the driveway; it must have been spring. The sky was singing and the air smelled of fresh cut Mexican Marigold. As I walked toward the backyard I could feel my soft socks pushing into the soles of my shoes, my heels pressing against the cold concrete. My mother was standing in the shade of the garage sorting clothes from the dryer. She was smiling as I approached. I had something to tell her when our attention was stolen by the sound of our kitchen door closing, followed by the rusty spring from our screen door snapping shut. We both turned to see my father walking toward us, his slight step down that small ledge after our side entrance welcome mat. He was proud of me and he wanted to be by my side as I shared the good news.

My father looked younger than his age. His complexion was rosy like he had been working in the garden. His hair, absent the gray that had sprung forth from worry, reflected richly in the season sun.

His stride was strong. He didn't rely on a cane or his walker. With his chest proudly pushed in front of him, guiding his gentle gate, and his slim shoulders were tight, rigid, and pulled back. The struggles of this past year seemed distant as the sturdy strength in his legs lunged with confidence.

I wished my brother were there to witness. I was relieved to see my father so happy when he suddenly skipped a short step and his balance wavered.

I rushed toward him with great concern, my arms reached for his body, helped to hold him straight, and attempted to adjust his staggering stance. With my hands pressed against his chest I could feel his fragile bones bending and his heart slowly beating.

My support turned into an embrace as his body went numb; his head rested on my shoulder as I screamed to my mother for help. He was heavy as his weight pushed upon me. He looked at me with a fear I had never seen. His pupils were dilated, spilling a deep gray that blackened his bright blue eyes. I could feel his rib cage expanding as he took a deep breath. His lips trembled, his mouth seemed impossibly dry. I had never seen my father so scared.

A rousing rush of energy abandoned my body leaving me trembling as I woke. I couldn't find my breath. My eyes wouldn't stop watering. Dark was my bedroom—waiting for sunlight. It was 5:03 in the morning.

Kevin Staniec is an arts advocate, author, and publisher. He holds a degree in Creative Writing and Film & Media Arts from Chapman University and has worked at the Autry National Center, Muckenthaler Cultural Center, and the Orange County Museum of Art. He currently programs the Arts, Culture, and Education division at the Orange County Great Park.

In 2002, Kevin co-founded ISM, a non-profit organization publishing paperback projects and producing international art experiments. In 2013, Kevin co-founded Black Hill Press, a publishing collective dedicated to the novella. He has produced exhibitions and programs with many institutions including Bergamot Station Arts Center, Grand Central Art Center, Laguna Art Museum, Long Beach Museum of Art, and the Orange County Center for Contemporary Art.

Kevin is the author of *And This Was My Happy Ending, I Am. You Are.*, *The Adventures of Super Bunny and Giant Cat Bear and Charlie*, *How to Catch a Cloud*, *How to be a Super Hero*, and *Begin*.

Sami Viljanto is from Helsinki, Finland. He graduated from Helsinki Polytechnic with a BA in New Media Design in 2008 and rather than following his course alumni into careers in web development decided to listen to his heart and pursue a career in Illustration, and judging by his output since, we think it fair to say he made the right decision.

Illustration offered Sami the chance to allow his creative tendencies to run riot, in 2010 he formed his own illustration company called Grande Deluxe which has worked on a variety of commercial projects for a variety of clients, among them; Uplause, Plan Finland, Päivi Raivio and Göoo Magazine.

William recently relocated to breathtaking and traffic-free Athens, Georgia, from back-breaking and happiness-eviscerating Los Angeles, California, where he came mercifully close to making a living as a hired gun writing and editing copy for various commercial enterprises and creative endeavors. He began his lifelong roadtrip in the deprecated sands of Las Vegas, Nevada, and as a result of a military patriarch, and a subsequent unabated restlessness, has changed addresses fifty-six times in thirty-eight years. Fearing for his alleged future he succumbed to a degree in Graphic Design, which proved a path of minor resistance, and by no means a door-opening maneuver.

William's synaptic meanderings have appeared on his website (agentofdiscord.com) and: in technical form on WIRED.com and THALO.com, in novella form in Silence (Transplant Press – 2000), in memoir/novel form in A Selfish Man (Publish America – 2003), in short story form in Rain Crow Magazine (Athens Diptych – Issue #3), will appear again next year in short story form in an anthology supporting the non-profit Mines Advisory Group (The Atlantic – 2013), and finally, in voluminous letters to persons still enchanted with non-electronic communication. PS they almost never write back…